Not I, Not I

A Follett JUST Beginning-To-Read Book

Not I, Not I

Margaret Hillert

Illustrated by Diana Magnuson

FOLLETT PUBLISHING COMPANY
Chicago

Library of Congress Cataloging in Publication Data

Hillert, Margaret.
Not I, not I.

(Follett just beginning-to-read books)
SUMMARY: The little red hen finds none of her lazy friends willing to help her plant, harvest, or grind wheat into flour, but all are eager to eat the bread she makes from it.
[1. Folklore] I. Magnuson, Diana. II. Title. III. Title: Little red hen.
PZ8.1.H539No 398.2'452'861 [E] 79-23847
ISBN 0-695-41353-8 lib. bdg.
ISBN 0-695-31353-3 pbk.

Library of Congress Catalog Card Number: 79-23847

International Standard Book Number: 0-695-41353-8 Library binding
0-695-31353-3 Paper binding

First Printing

Here is a mother.
The mother is little.
The mother is red.

Look here.
Here is a little baby.
The baby is yellow.
It can run and play.

See the yellow baby run.
See it run to Mother.
It said, "Mother, Mother.
I want something."

Mother said, "Come and look.
Help me find something.
Away we go."

Look, look.
Here is something.
Something little.
I can work.
I can make it big.

Oh, oh.
Look here.
One, two, three.
Can you help me?

Not I.
Not I.
Not I.
We can not help.

I can.
I can work.
See it go down here.

Look, look.
See where it is.
It is up.
It is big, big, big.

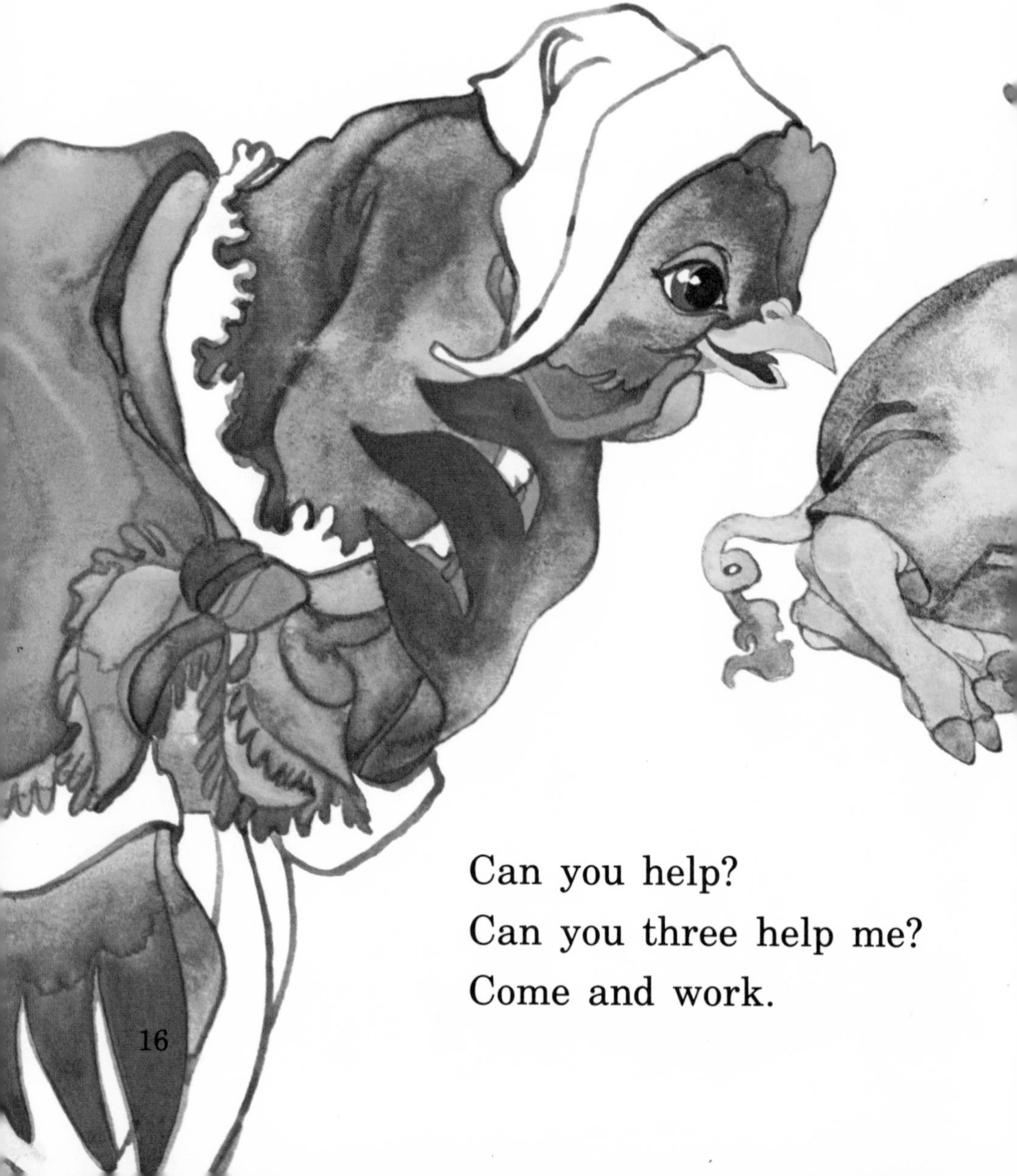

Can you help?
Can you three help me?
Come and work.

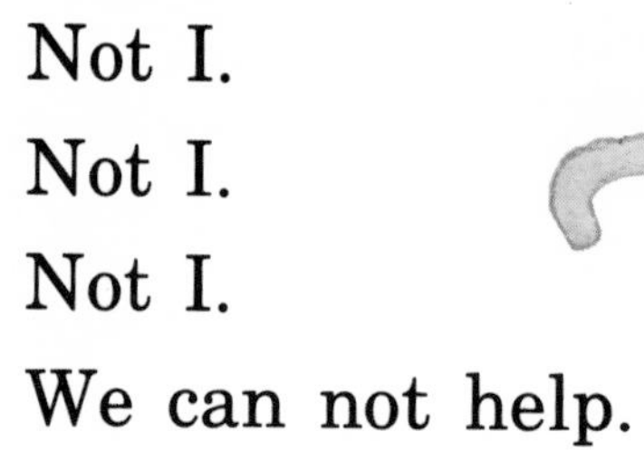

Not I.
Not I.
Not I.
We can not help.

It is funny.
You can not work.
You can not help.
I can work.

Here I go.
Away, away.
Can you come?
Can you help?

Not I.
Not I.
Not I.
We can not help.

See, see.
It is in here.
I can make something.

I can work.
See me work.
I can make something.

Look here, baby.
It can go in here.
It is for you.

Here it is.
Come and look.
Oh, oh.
Can you help me?

I can.
I can.
I can.
We can help.

Oh, oh.
We see it.
We want it.

Not you.
Not you.
Not you.
Go away.
It is for my little baby and me.

Margaret Hillert, author of many Follett JUST Beginning-To-Read Books, has been a first-grade teacher in Royal Oak, Michigan, since 1948.

Not I, Not I uses the 44 words listed below.

a
and
away

baby
big

can
come

down

find
for
funny

go

help
here

I
in
is
it

little
look

make
me
mother
my

not

oh
one

play

red
run

said
see
something

the
three
to
two

up

want
we
where
work

yellow
you